Fred the Fox Shouts "NO!"

By Tatiana Y. Kisil Matthews • Illustrated by Allison Fears

To my mom who always asked me,
"What do you think?"
- TKM

Always believe in yourself.
- AZF

To MHO who helped get the
wheels turning!
-AZF
-TKM

Dear Family and Friends of Little Ones,

This book is intended to be an interactive experience. It is our attempt to make a tough conversation a little easier. Many of us would like to believe that the biggest threat to our children is "stranger danger." Unfortunately, the reality is that the biggest threat comes from people whom they know. It is not a child's responsibility to protect themselves from adults. However, if we can empower our children to use their voices, trust their instincts, and know they have personal rights, maybe we can protect just one. That's our responsibility.

Thanks for taking the time to read this to the ones you love.

Tatiana Matthews and Allison Fears

Hi! My name is Fred, and I live on the edge of a quiet path in a lovely part of the woods with my fox family.

My mommy, daddy, baby sister, and I have a warm and cozy den away from the hustle and bustle of the busy forest life. I have lots of friends who live near me. I enjoy the school I go to. I am very happy with my soccer team and church friends.

My parents have spoken with me many times about safety with strangers. Something we have not talked about is safety with people I know.

One morning, my mom and dad told me that they heard some very sad news about an adult they trusted. This adult touched children on parts of their body that are private.

I asked them to explain to me what "private" means.

Do you know what "PRIVATE" means?

My mom said, "Private is something special that only you need to see or know about."

"Parts of our body are private because they are special," said Dad.

"So I'm in charge of my private parts?" I asked.

"Yes, that's right!" said Mom. "You are in charge of your private parts."

"There are times when adults, whom you have asked for help, see your private parts," Mom explained.

"You mean like when I ask Mom for help after I use the potty?"

"That's right," said Mom and Dad.

"What about when I'm at the doctor's office?" I wondered.

"That's okay only when Mom or Dad is with you and you give your permission," said Mom.

8

Who might see your private areas
in order to help you?
WHEN WOULD IT BE OKAY?

Mom and Dad told me that the adult who had touched those children on their private parts did a very bad thing.

Mom asked me, "What would you do if an adult or older kid asked to touch your private parts?"

I told them really loud and mean, "I'd say no!"

What would you say?
Can you say it really
LOUD AND MEAN?

Then they asked me, "What would you do if that person tried to touch your private parts without asking?"

I told them even louder and meaner, "I'd say no!"

What would you say?
Can you say it even
LOUDER AND MEANER?

Then my mom and dad asked me, "What if they told you if you touched their private parts it would give you magic powers?"
Screaming as loud as I could, I said, "I'd say no!"

What would you say?
Can you SCREAM IT
as loud as you can?

After that question they asked, "What if they offered you lots of your favorite candy?"

I shouted back, "I'd say no!"

18

What would you say?
Can you SHOUT IT back?

My mom and dad got very serious when they asked me the next question. "What if someone said they would hurt you or your family if you ever told anyone? Would you keep that secret?"

I shouted, "No, no, no! I wouldn't keep that secret. I know you would protect me and I would never get in trouble!"

20

What would you say?
Can you SHOUT IT OUT?

I told my mom and dad, "I really liked practicing how to keep myself safe. I especially liked yelling as loud as I could!"

Mom and Dad told me that just because someone is older than you, it does not mean they can do whatever they want.

If I feel yucky about something an adult or big kid is saying or
doing, I can say no and go talk to my mommy and daddy. I always
have Mommy and Daddy on my team. I can even go tell a teacher,
policeman, or any adult that helps keep me safe!

I asked my mom and dad, "Does this mean that I can tell my babysitter that I am not going to bed tonight when you are at the movies?"

This time my mom and dad said, "No!"

THE END

ABOUT THE AUTHOR

Tatiana Matthews is a practicing Licensed Professional Counselor with 13 years of clinical experience treating adults and adolescents in the wealthiest county of Georgia. Despite the economic advantage of this community, the pattern of victims knowing their offenders and the majority of victims never reporting the abuse remains true. Through this experience, Tatiana identified the need to increase parent and child dialogue about sexual abuse prevention. Tatiana resides in Dunwoody, GA with her husband Jim, their two children Maximus and Luna and their two Chesapeake Bay Retrievers Beacon and Bay.

ABOUT THE ILLUSTRATOR

Allison Fears is a graduate of The University of North Carolina at Chapel Hill who worked for many years in the advertising industry. She left her demanding career in 2006 to take on the even more demanding career of motherhood. A life long, self-proclaimed "doodler," Allison had frequently daydreamed about illustrating a children's book of her own. When approached with the story line for Fred the Fox, Allison's creativity was sparked by her passion for her own children's safety and the safety of all children. Allison resides in Dunwoody, GA with her husband Taylor, their two children Carter and Elli and their dog Bennet.

Made in the USA
Lexington, KY
01 October 2013